COMET
SECOND BASE
ffron
Greyhound

SANDY
PITCHER
Ronnie
Silver Lab

KOKO
CENTER FIELD
W9-AMA-639
Coltrane
Siberian Husky /
Wolf Dog Mix

DUKE
CATCHER
out
German Shepherd

PEEWEE
LEFT FIELD
Lola
Black Lab /
Pit Bull / Husky Mix

MAX
RIGHT FIELD
Maxwell
Boxer

BUSTER
THIRD BASE
ue
Pit Bull Mix

SCOOTER
FIRST BASE
Einstein
Rhodesian
Ridgeback

RED
SHORTSTOP
Rudy
Hound / Pit Bull Mix

Hounds

To the real Casey—our star!

Text and illustrations copyright © 2012 by Diane deGroat and Shelley Rotner

All rights reserved. Published by Orchard Books, an imprint of Scholastic Inc., *Publishers since 1920.* ORCHARD BOOKS and design are registered trademarks of Watts Publishing Group, Ltd., used under license. SCHOLASTIC and associated logos are trademarks and/or registered trademarks of Scholastic Inc. No part of this publication may be reproduced, stored in a retrieval system, or transmitted in any form or by any means, electronic, mechanical, photocopying, recording, or otherwise, without written permission of the publisher. For information regarding permission, write to Orchard Books, Scholastic Inc., Permissions Department, 557 Broadway, New York, NY 10012.

Library of Congress Cataloging-in-Publication Data
de Groat, Diane. Homer / Diane deGroat and Shelley Rotner —1st ed. p. cm.
Summary: While Alex sleeps, his dog Homer dreams about the game that will determine whether his team, the Doggers, or their opponents, the Hounds, will be champions of the world of dog baseball. [1. Baseball—Fiction. 2. Dogs—Fiction. 3. Dreams—Fiction.] I. Rotner, Shelley. II. Title. PZ7.D3639Hom 2012 [E]—dc23 2011015272

ISBN 978-0-545-33272-9 • 10 9 8 7 6 5 4 3 2 1   12 13 14 15 16 • Printed in Singapore 46 • First edition, March 2012

The display type was set in San Remo Casual. The text was set in Archer Medium. The art was created using photographs and digital art. Book design by Becky Terhune

We would like to acknowledge the many dogs who sat, stood, and howled their way into our hearts, as well as their owners for their patience, sense of humor, and willingness to try the impossible. We are also grateful to Alison Smith at Paradox Breeder and to Biscuit and Bath in New York City. A special thanks goes to Gabriel. Dog lovers are a special breed!

—D.D. & S.R.

Homer

DIANE deGROAT and SHELLEY ROTNER

ORCHARD BOOKS
NEW YORK
AN IMPRINT OF SCHOLASTIC INC.

Alex loved baseball. Homer did, too.
They even dreamed of baseball.

Then, one special night . . .

. . . Homer met his friends at the baseball field for the big game.

The locker room was wagging with excitement.

Who will be the champions?
The Hounds or the Doggers?

The Doggers take the field.

The fans yip and yowl for the home team.

The Hounds score a run in the first inning . . .

. . . and two more in the second!

But the Doggers can't even get a hit!

At the bottom of the ninth, the Doggers are down 3 to 0.
Dizzy strikes out!
Will the Doggers ever catch up?

It's the last chance for the Doggers.
Rocket steps up to the plate. He hits a single!

Next up is Whitey. He walks!

Lucky hits a droolball!

The Doggers' luck is changing!
The crowd goes wild!

Now it's up to Homer. Can he do it?

STRIKE ONE!
THE CROWD GROANS.

STRIKE TWO!
THE CROWD MOANS.
HOMER
1
DUKE
12

Bases loaded!
Two strikes. The pressure is on!

HERE'S THE PITCH . . . HE SWINGS!
IT'S A LONG DRIVE TO CENTER FIELD! IT'S WAAAY BACK!
THAT BALL IS GOING . . . GOING . . . IT'S GONE!
VISITOR: HOUNDS
START TIME: MIDNIGHT
HOME: DOGGERS
END TIME:
BEAR

Grand slam! The Doggers win—4 to 3!
They are the new champions!

What a game!